P9-DIY-379

Henry Holt and Company   New York

MAHOPAC FALLS
SCHOOL LIBRARY

The Maestro Plays

by Bill Martin Jr

pictures by
Vladimir Radunsky

THE MAESTRO PLAYS.
HE PLAYS PROUDLY.
HE PLAYS LOUDLY.

He plays slowly

He plays oh..ly.

He plays reachingly.

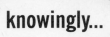

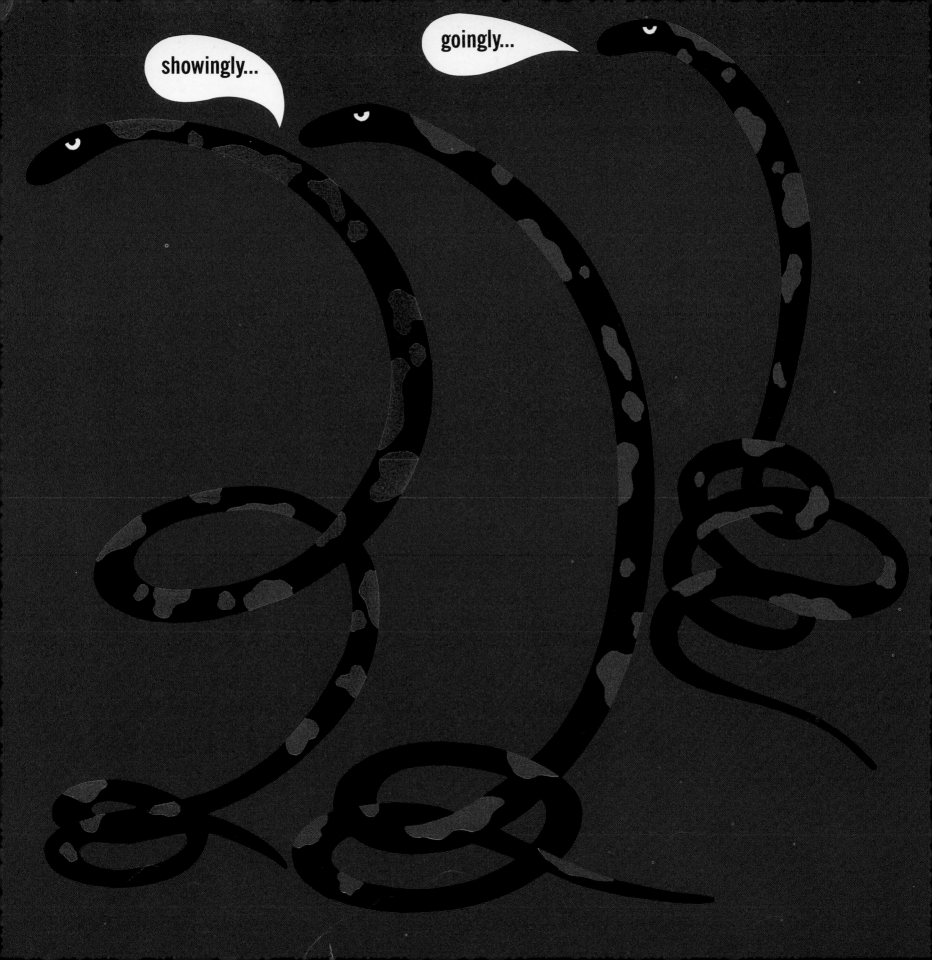

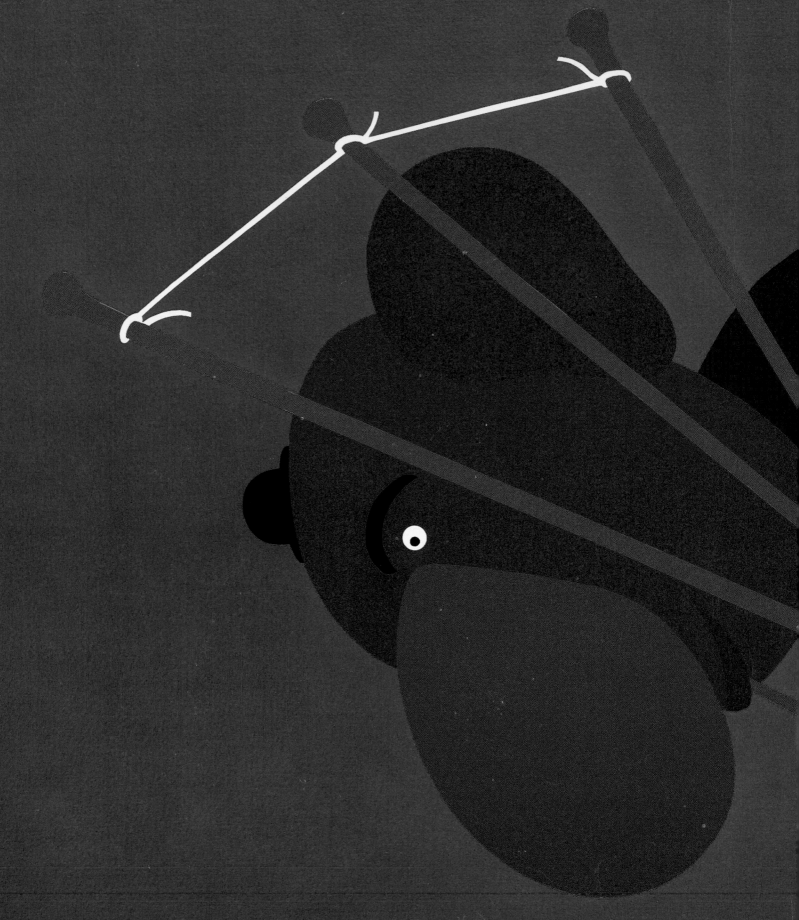

Now he he is playing singingly.

He is playing ringingly,

wingingly . . .

swingingly

flingingly

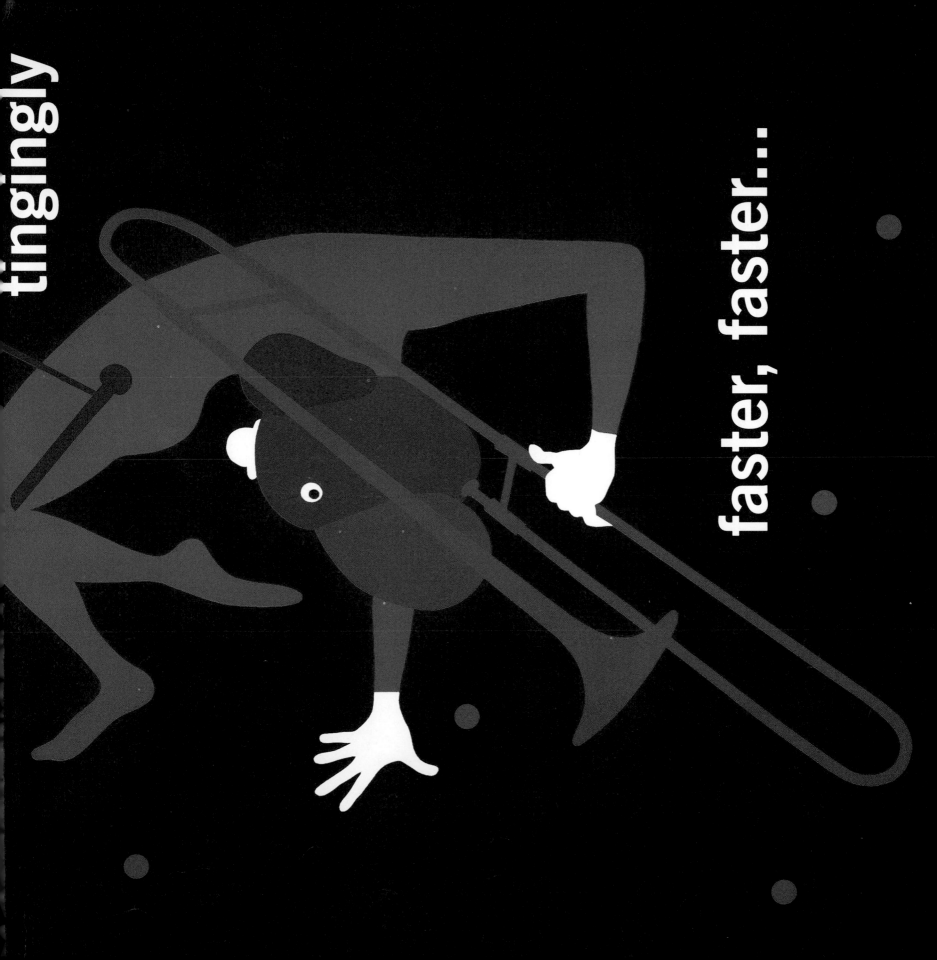

He plays busily.

He plays

dizzily.

He stops. He mops his brow.

The maestro begins

playing again mildly....

But suddenly he's playing wildly...

He bows furiously

He jabs!

He stabs!

He saws!

He slaps the strings.

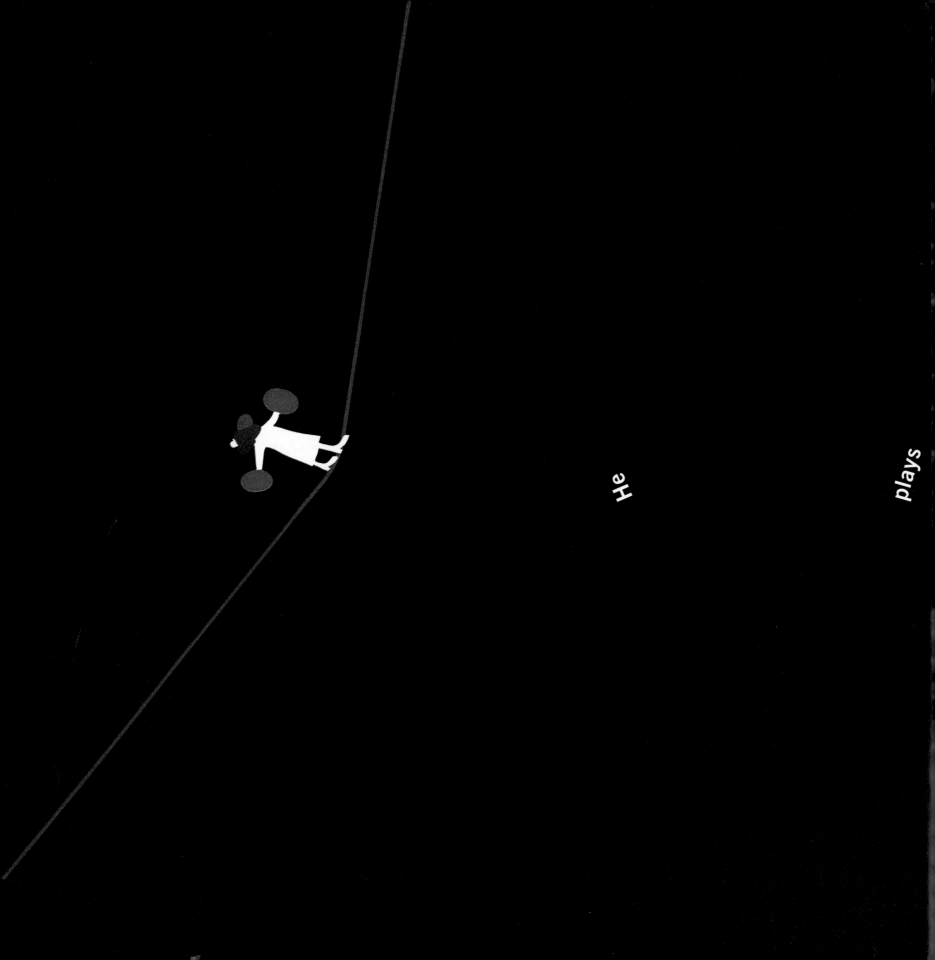

He

plays

trrrr-r-r-r-ippingly.

He plays skippingly...

He plays sweepingly...
leapingly...
cheepingly...
faster...
faster.

He plays nippingly,

drippingly...

zippingly...

clippingly...

pippingly...

Rrrrriiiiiiiiipppppiiinngly...

The concert is
over.

CLAP

BRAVO! BRAVO!

CLAP

E
MAR

Martin, Bill F-19295

The maestro plays C2

$15.45

DATE OCT 17			
JAN 1 0	NOV 15	20M 1C	71C
AUG 1 1			AP 21
NOV 9	NOV 22	FEB 4	
DEC 7	MAY 26	FEB 2	
OCT 4		APR 8	
		2CR	
NOV 7		2-2M	
1C		DE 17 '99	

LIBRARY
FULMAR ROAD SCHOOL
MAHOPAC, N.Y. 10541
C2
WITHDRAWN

FULMAR ROAD ELEM SCH/LIBY
FULMAR ROAD
MAHOPAC NY 10541

12/01/1994

MAHOPAC FALLS
SCHOOL LIBRARY

BAKER & TAYLOR BOOKS